Disney · PIXAR
Cars

# Home Sweet Home

ADVANCE
PUBLISHERS

Exciting things were happening in Radiator Springs. Now that Lightning McQueen had opened his racing headquarters, the town was flooded with tourists.

"Boy, this place is really jumpin'," said Lightning.

Radiator Springs was back on the map!

Cars were lining up around the block to buy new tires from Luigi. His assistant, Guido, was the fastest tire changer in Carburetor County, but even he couldn't keep up. Luigi was starting to wonder if they were too busy.

Next door, Lizzie had fallen asleep while customers were waiting to get into her shop. She was happy to be selling her bumper stickers, but she was also just plain exhausted.

Big hearted and excitable, Luigi's enthusiasm and energy rubs off on everyone around him. He couldn't wait to fit out Lightning McQueen in a set of new whitewall tires.

MOTELFULL
TENTS
AVAILABLE

Every shop in town was
jammed. Flo's V8 Café was
so busy that Lightning offered
to help serve the customers. The
visiting cars were thrilled to have
Lightning McQueen as their waiter!
　　At her motel, Sally had more customers than
she had rooms. Sarge loaned Sally some army surplus tents.

This town is too busy!" Sally
exclaimed. "I think we need a
town meeting. Lightning, can you
get everyone together?"
"Sure," Lightning said with a yawn.

The shop owners of Radiator Springs gathered in front of Luigi's tire store.

"Friends and neighbors," began Sally, "Radiator Springs is once again a busy and important town. We're a success!"

"That's great," said Ramone. "But I'm so busy I haven't painted myself in a week!"

"We need to chill," said Fillmore, "relax a little."

Just then, Lightning noticed that Lizzie looked like she was shivering. "Sally, it's cold out here," he said. "Can we take this meeting into the courthouse?"

Lizzie believes in telling it like it is. Her out-of-the-blue, straight-talking comments often surprise the younger inhabitants of Radiator Springs.

The courthouse was warm and toasty.

"Sally," said Mater, "will you tell us a bedtime story?"

"A bedtime story?" Sally said, laughing. "What kind of story?"

"Well, I'm still pretty new here," said Lightning. "Tell us about the early days of Radiator Springs. How did it all begin?"

"Oh, Lizzie should tell that story," said Sally. "After all, she knew Stanley best."

"She's resting," whispered Flo. "Go on. Tell it. Start with Stanley."

Sally smiled. "All right, everyone comfy?"

All the cars sleepily murmured, "Yes."

"Then let's begin," said Sally.

"Once upon a time, there was a big desert," said Sally. "There wasn't a place in sight for cars to stop for water and oil. That all changed when a clever car named Stanley discovered a bubbling natural spring. He filled his radiator with cool, refreshing water. Then he had a great idea! He would open up a shop that would service overheated travelers. He named the new settlement Radiator Springs. Stanley soon built a few other buildings, including an oil change station.

"One day, a lovely Model T named Lizzie rolled into town. It was love at first sight for Stanley. He convinced Lizzie to stay. So Lizzie took over the curios shop and began selling bumper stickers."

CURIOS

CURIOS

CURIOS

Lightning McQueen is fascinated by Lizzie's motoring bric-a-brac, such as bumper stickers and souvenir snow globes.

Flo yawned and smiled. "Sally, tell us how Stanley ended up on that rock in the center of town."

"Oh, that's a funny story," said Sally. "One day, while Stanley and Lizzie were scouting out nearby locations for new shops, a dust devil whipped right through the desert."

"A dust devil!" exclaimed Mater with a shiver. "That's almost as scary as the Ghost Light!"

"No, Mater," said Sally reassuringly. "A dust devil is just a small tornado. And the one that blew through the desert that day was pretty strong. It blew Stanley high up into the air and dropped him on top of a rock—the same rock that Stanley's statue sits on today."

When Lizzie thinks about the old times, she visits the statue of Stanley, the town's founder. She wishes Stanley could see how happy the town became after the new road was built.

Sally looked around the room. She was surprised
everyone was still awake.

"Keep going," said Lightning. "This is great!"

"All right," Sally said brightly. "Before long, Stanley and Lizzie expanded their little settlement. Lizzie opened a larger curios shop in the heart of town. And soon other shops and services were built, including a tire shop, a paint shop, and a café. Just about every car that traveled down Route 66 stopped by Radiator Springs. Even back then, it was a real friendly place."

"Then I settled here," said Doc, picking up the story from Sally. "I was looking for a quiet place to start over and Radiator Springs looked just right."

Doc told the story of how a rich cruiser from Las Vegas opened up the Wheel Well Motel up on the hill.

"Holy smokes, that was some fancy place," said Doc. "We even had the governor come spend the night."

"That's when we knew we were a proper town," said Sheriff proudly.

As well as looking after the townsfolk's health, Doc also looks after the law in Radiator Springs as the firm-but-fair town judge.

"The town was growing," said Sheriff.
"So we elected a sheriff—Me! And I got
Red to move here from out of state.
After all, every town needs a firefighter."

Sheriff explained how it took a while for the townsfolk to get used to Red. He was so shy and quiet! But they soon learned that whenever they needed help, Red was there for them.

Red is Radiator Springs' only fire truck. Red might be shy, but he also has a lot of friends around town who feel very protective toward him.

"The growing town needed a tow truck!" Mater shouted.

"That's right," said Sheriff. "When Mater first came to Radiator Springs, he was just passing through. But Luigi and Guido and Flo made him feel so welcome that Mater stayed."

"Tow-Mater Towing, at your service," Mater declared.

"Mater was so friendly," said Doc. "He charmed all of our visitors."

"Including me!" said Lightning.

His buddy Mater grinned happily.

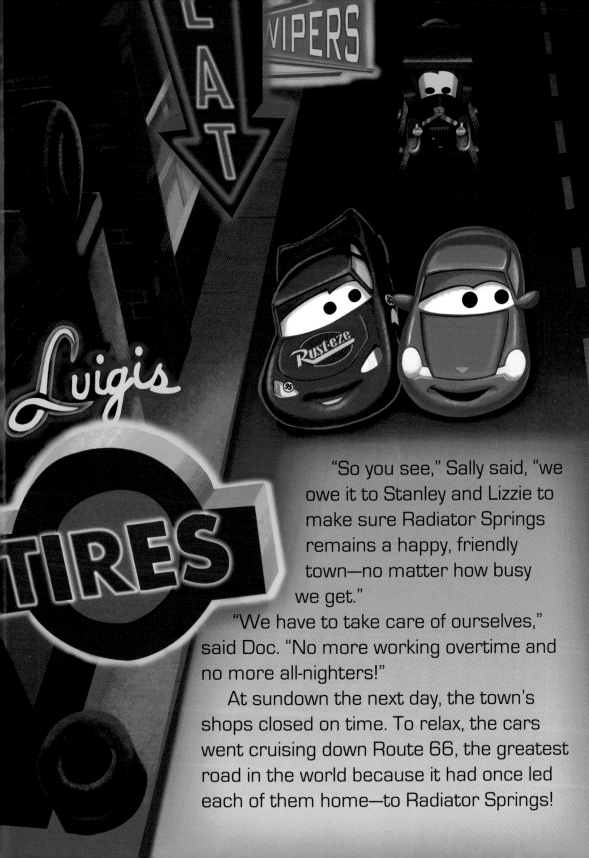

"So you see," Sally said, "we owe it to Stanley and Lizzie to make sure Radiator Springs remains a happy, friendly town—no matter how busy we get."

"We have to take care of ourselves," said Doc. "No more working overtime and no more all-nighters!"

At sundown the next day, the town's shops closed on time. To relax, the cars went cruising down Route 66, the greatest road in the world because it had once led each of them home—to Radiator Springs!

# JOKES
## RIDDLES
## SILLY STUFF

*Did you get them all right?*

| | |
|---|---|
| **CUL8R** | **O2BME** |
| See you later | Oh to be me |
| **12RACE** | **4U2C** |
| One to race | For you to see |
| **O2BINLA** | **GOOD2GO** |
| Oh to be in LA | Good to go |
| **URGR8** | **2QIK4U** |
| You're great | Too quick for you |
| **LV2RACE** | **LOWNSLO** |
| Love to race | Low and slow |
| **WINR** | **L8RGATR** |
| Winner | Later gator |
| **MT TANK** | **CAR MD** |
| Empty tank | Car doctor |

**Which cars start with a T?**
*None. They all start with gas!*

**What did the first stoplight say to the second stoplight?**
*Don't look now. I'm changing!*

**What do you get when you put a car and a pet together?**
*Carpet*

**What is the difference between a flashing red traffic light and a flashing yellow traffic light?**
*The color*

**Where does a car swim?**
*In a car pool*

**What did Mater say to the fence post?**
*I never expected to run into you.*

**Where will you find roads without cars, forests without trees and cities without houses?**
*On a map*

**The traffic sign read, "Railroad Crossing, Look out for the Cars." Can you spell that, without any R's?**
*T-h-a-t.*

**FILLMORE'S WOES:**
*You know you are an old bus . . .*
if you give high fives when passing another car . . . uphill.

*You know you are an old bus . . .*
if every time someone reaches for the sliding door handle you start to panic and yell "Be careful, that comes right off."

*You know you are an old bus . . .*
if you carry a towel with you to wipe the windshield because your defroster doesn't work.

*You know you are an old bus . . .*
if you are serious about your," Honk if Anything Falls Off!" bumper sticker.

*You know you are an old bus . . .*
if every time you pass a junk yard, you wonder if they have the parts you need.

**Why did Fillmore stop in the middle of the road?**
*He was wheely, wheely tired.*

**"Take the wheel, Honey!" said the nervous driver.**
*"There's a tree coming straight for us!"*

**How many wheels should a car have?**
*5 . . . 4 wheels and 1 steering wheel.*

**How many words can you make from RADIATOR SPRINGS?**

_____
_____
_____

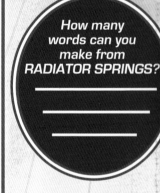